MW01675844

A Black Cat Named SMOKEY On Vacation

Story & Drawings by
ROBYN DEAN

ZYXALON PRESS MINNEAPOLIS

Copyright © 1992 by Robyn Dean

All rights reserved.

Published in the United States by ZYXALON Press.

First Edition, Second Printing

ISBN 0-9633466-0-1

Library of Congress Catalog Card Number: 92-93502

ZYXALON PRESS MINNEAPOLIS

Printed in U.S.A.

A Black Cat Named

SMOKEY ON VACATION

Story & Drawings By

ROBYN DEAN

Smokey was a big, black cat.
His life had no upsets.
He played and purred the whole day long,
Loved tuna, treats and pets.

TUNA

A sweeter cat than dear old Smoke,
Did not exist in town.
His face was flat, his fur was long,
His eyes glowed copper-brown.

Then one fine day while Smokey played
His friends all formed a plan.
A trip was laid for mountain days
For Susan, Kent and Dan.

Without a hint of what-was-what,
They packed up Smokey's toys.
They took the black cat far away
And sang out with great noise:

"So long," they cried. "Have fun! Don't sigh!
We'll see you in a week.
Now don't you fret 'cause we'll just bet,
You'll have games of hide-and-seek!"

Welcome
Kent—
Just leave
the cat
anywhere.
Have a
fun trip!
Love, Aunt
Grace

So out they went with boots and tents,
The mountain trails to see,
While Smokey sniffed at foreign airs
And wondered, "What of me?"

The first thing that sweet Smokey did,
Was take a look about.
The house was big and dark and drear.
The silence seemed to shout.

First he found some crooked stairs,
Down which he trod his paws.

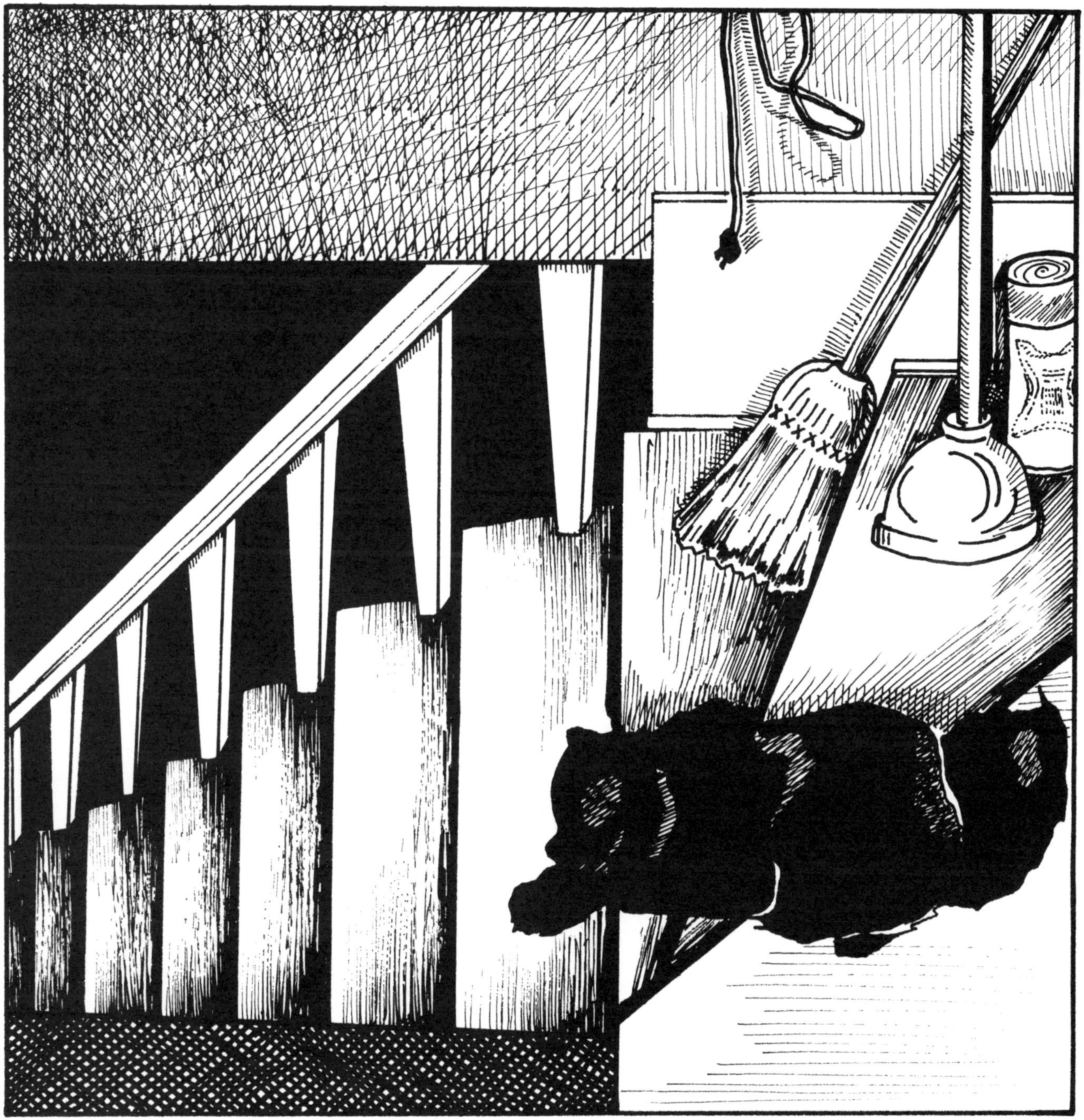

He caught a glimpse of tiny nymphs
And cobwebs made of gauze.

The next new room he came to view,
He met a big surprise.
A tabby cat with long nose sat
And stared into his eyes.

That day Smoke vowed he'd never bow
To any cat with stripes.
He kept open eyes and stayed near by,
As if he knew this type.

The funny part about this lark
Was that Smokey was so sweet.
He'd never met another pet
And so his threats were meek.

When bedtime came that first late night,
An anxious cat was found.
He could not rest within that house
Where dangers did abound.

He sought a place, tucked in with Grace.
Perhaps with her was best?
But Grace was not so pleased to spot
A cat within her nest.

He liked the next room's friendly warmth,
Away from danger's jaws.

But waterbeds and cats don't mix –
Because of those sharp claws!

"They said I'd love this new-found home
And that I should not fret –
But this is not the same fun game
Of tuna, treats and pets!"

He wondered if his so-called friends
Were camping out all right.
He hoped they'd freeze and eat some weeds,
Meet grizzly bears at night!

In fact, the three that camped by trees
Were happy in the woods.
Each one agreed, most hopefully,
The cat had understood.

As much as they all loved dear Smoke,
They knew he was not right
For pitching tents with tree boughs bent
And moonlit, campfire nights.

"Imagine him with us," they laughed,
"When critters play and prowl.
Imagine Smokey's shuddering fright
When coyotes start to howl!"

AH-WOOOOOO!
AH-WOOOOOOOOO..

"If we took Smokey up atop
The mountain trails we track,
I don't think he'd be very pleased
Being strapped to someone's back!"

These were the jokes Smoke's friends did tell
Along their woodsy trail
Though toward the end, they did admit
They missed his fluffy tail.

"Now, a more handsome cat than he
I doubt we'd ever find.
Oh, sweet! Oh, soft! Oh, nice to pet!
For him I do so pine!"

“So let us fly straight home,” they cried,
“And fetch that big, black cat
Who must be now a-wanting so
To greet his friends and chat.”

With that they flew, that merry crew,
Their fluffy cat to get.
To hug him, squeeze him, love him up,
With tuna, treats, and pets.

As soon-as-soon, the three arrived
And rushed up to the door.
Sweet Smoke was waiting there and gave
A happy, yelping roar!

"Hooray! I'm saved," the black cat raved.
"That was a nasty trick,
To leave me grieving all alone.
Good gosh, I was homesick!"

They said with glee, "Oh, Dear Smokey,
We love you to the core!
We hope you're happy to go home
To tuna, treats and more!"

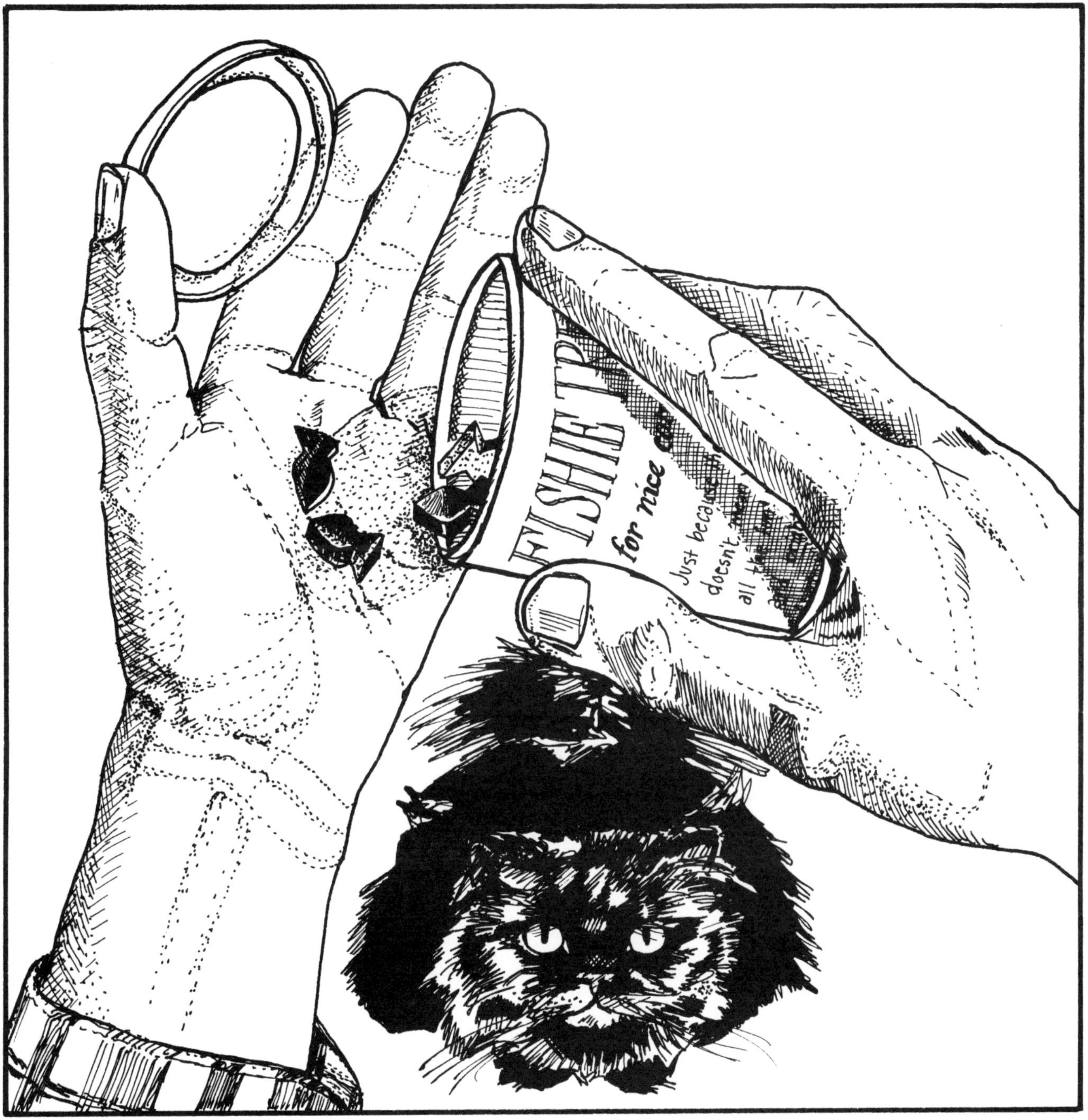
for nice

They fed him, pet him, loved him up,
But then they had to note;
A much exhausted cat he was,
With scruffy, dusty coat.

"Poor thing! Indeed, a BATH he needs,
Although he hates the wet.
But don't despair, we'll make it up,
With tuna, treats and pets!"

SMOKEY
is a Persian cat. He is entirely black from a group called TEDDY BEAR CATS. They are known to be gentle and playful all of their lives. Persian cats are bred for their flat faces and long, silky fur. These cats must be groomed and bathed regularly which creates a unique relationship between cat and owner.

ROBYN DEAN
has always been awed by the apparent serenity of animals and likes to imagine what they are thinking. *A Black Cat Named Smokey: On Vacation* is her first book. Ms. Dean is a graphic designer and lives in Minneapolis, Minnesota.